The Curse of Claudia

The Curse of CLAUDIA

Edward Miller

Crown Publishers, Inc.
New York

to Jenny Marie Mastrarrigo

Copyright © 1989 by Edward Miller III
All rights reserved. No part of this book may be reproduced or transmitted in
any form or by any means, electronic or mechanical, including
photocopying, recording, or by any information storage and retrieval system,
without permission in writing from the publisher.
Published by Crown Publishers, Inc., 225 Park Avenue South, New York,
New York 10003.
CROWN is a trademark of Crown Publishers, Inc.
Manufactured in the United States of America

Library of Congress Cataloging-in-Publication Data
Miller, Edward (Edward Ward) The curse of Claudia/Edward Miller.
Summary: Claudia visits her old high school friend Eva the zombie in
Dracula's castle and drastically changes the lives of all the monsters staying
there.
[1. Monsters—Fiction.] I. Title. PZ7.M61286Cu 1989   [E]—dc19
89-1522   CIP
ISBN 0-517-57408-X
ISBN 0-517-57409-8 (lib. bdg.)

10 9 8 7 6 5 4 3 2 1

First Edition

It was a dark and gloomy night—perfect for a vampire bat like me to take a stroll—when to my surprise, an unexpected guest came to pay us a visit.

I quickly flew inside and changed to answer the door. It was Claudia, a high school friend of Eva, the zombie. I shielded my eyes from her brightness.

Claudia sang their high
school cheer to announce
her arrival to Eva.

Hearing Claudia's obnoxious singing, Eva slowly descended the stairs to greet her old friend.

She was glad to see Claudia. I could tell because Eva's complexion turned a darker shade of green, the way it always does when she's happy.

Claudia remarked, "You know, a little fresh air would do wonders for you." They walked into the living room to reminisce about old times.

At six o'clock the next morning, Claudia came banging on my door. "Wake up, it's morning," she said. But I said, "Vampires sleep during the day." "No excuses," Claudia replied. "It's time for morning exercises."

Before I knew it she had
us all up and jogging around
the yard.

After our jog, I served lizards in slime sauce for breakfast. That was my revenge for being woken so early.

I was disturbed to see that she loved the lizards and wanted my recipe.

That afternoon I overheard Claudia talking to Barnabas, the gardener. She had plans to clean the garden as a surprise for Eva.

They moved the tombstones and planted a rock garden. They pulled out the weeds and planted ugly flowers in full bloom.

When Eva came out to see the surprise she screamed with fright. Barnabas remarked, ''That's the first time I ever saw Eva lose her composure.''

When Eva recovered,
Claudia decided to do
something about Eva's
greenish skin and hairdo.

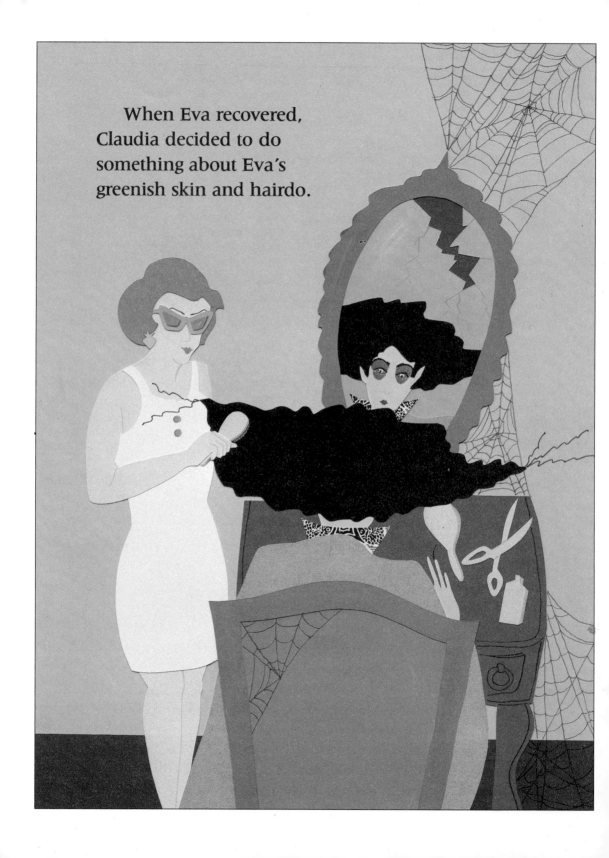

Four-and-a-half hours later Claudia was still making up Eva when I went in to take a peek.

What a gruesome sight!
Eva was relieved to know
that makeup washes off.
So was I.

After dinner it was my turn to get back at Claudia for scaring us all day. I invited some friends over to help me.

We all hid in the kitchen
waiting for her to return for
lizard leftovers.

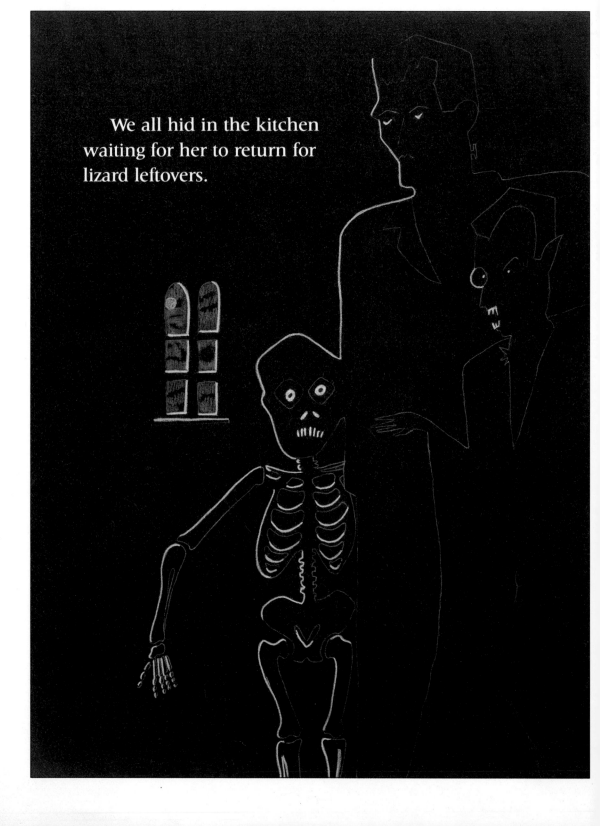

When she finally opened the door, everyone
yelled "Boo!"

"Oh!" screamed Claudia. "A surprise party
for me? I love it."

She instantly called some other high school friends to join the party. I made more lizards in slime sauce for the unexpected guests.

The party went on till all hours of the morning.
I couldn't understand how Eva could take it for so
long.

The following afternoon when we woke up Claudia was leaving. She had let us sleep through morning exercises.

I was relieved to see her go because she was the only human scarier than a monster.

Even after she left, she still managed to scare us one more time. She had been cleaning all day.

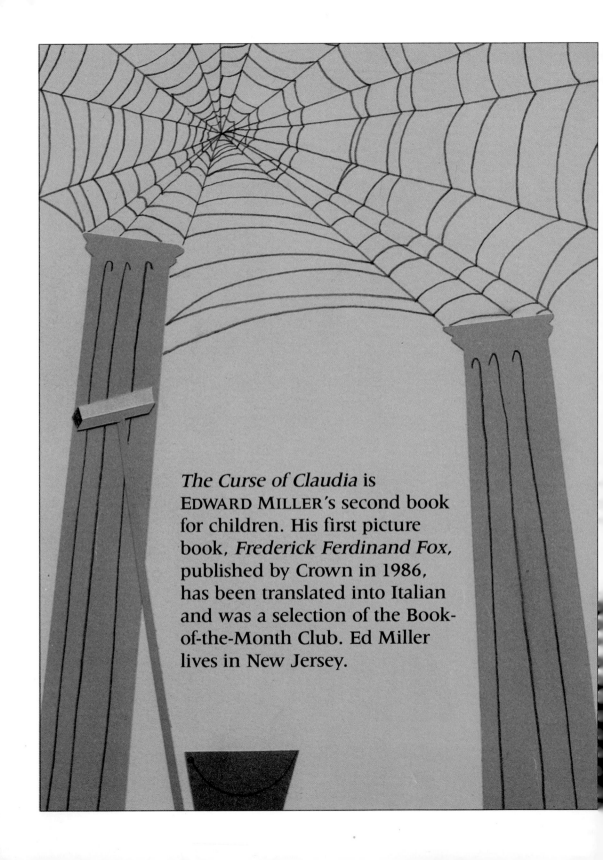

The Curse of Claudia is
EDWARD MILLER's second book
for children. His first picture
book, *Frederick Ferdinand Fox*,
published by Crown in 1986,
has been translated into Italian
and was a selection of the Book-
of-the-Month Club. Ed Miller
lives in New Jersey.